Rolling in Sin

A 1Night Stand Story

By
Kayleigh Malcolm

Copyright © 2016 by Kayleigh Malcolm
ISBN: 978-1-68361-013-7
Cover art by Mina Carter

Published by Decadent Publishing Company, LLC
Look for us online at:
www.decadentpublishing.com

~A Note from the Author~

I have always loved the concept of love at first sight and soul mates. Our enigmatic Madame Eve has the ability to match her clients up with their ideal partner and that appealed my everlasting romantic side, which in turn inspired my writing. I'm looking forward to exploring more of 1NS and the people who are appearing in my head looking for one night but deep down want forever.

If you want to know more about my writing and general craziness, I can always be found on facebook or feel free to email me. I love to hear from my readers!

Kayleigh

https://www.facebook.com/kayleigh.malcolm.1
kmalcolmauthor@gmail.com

Dedication

I'm blessed to have many people in my corner encouraging me to follow my dreams. I can never thank you enough. XO

Chapter One

Audrey Leporte sat in her ergonomically correct chair, her heart beating so hard she feared the entire office might hear it. An email from her friend Joan sat open on her computer screen. She'd read it three times, just to make certain she hadn't misunderstood, and the anticipation and nerves kept her heart pounding.

I can't believe she really did it.

As often as their schedules allowed, Audrey and her best friends got together, but with each of them following different career paths, their girls' nights were becoming fewer and further between. When they'd met for cocktail hour a couple of weeks before, they'd discussed having a weekend away in Las Vegas. It hadn't taken too many martinis before a discussion revolving around their deepest, darkest fantasies started, so they weren't the least bit surprised to discover they shared another common bond of sexual fantasies. They planned to blow off a little steam and no one would be the wiser, thanks to that wonderful Vegas rule.

Not that Audrey thought she would do anything really wild—she rarely did, being the designated driver and mother hen who always ensured everyone got home safely. *But, if we're in Sin City, then maybe I can cut loose and have some fun. What happens in Vegas stays in Vegas.* She could live the fantasies she'd imagined while lying around in her practical pajamas, in her twin bed, in her miniscule apartment. What if, this once, she decided not to be practical?

Spending forty hours a week in a five-by-five foot square, virtually forgotten by her co-workers, she typed away, often through lunch. She'd never been late or phoned in sick and always met her deadlines. Her life was an endless series of columns and tallies, all in off-white and beige. Just like her wardrobe.

In an earlier email, Joan had mentioned a special dating service she'd heard about from friends, one that specialized in requests and would be perfect for their crazy weekend. Life had been one agonizingly boring, identical day after another, and a single web-link might change all that, at least for one night.

Trembling with excitement and casting a quick glance over her shoulder to ensure no one nosey stood nearby, Audrey typed out her reply:

I'm in.

***

From across the street, Audrey watched the phenomenal performance of the Bellagio fountain's timed music and water spray. Everything about Las Vegas fascinated her. She'd never seen so much flashing neon or such a vast array of wild-acting people in one place before. She hardly remembered anything she or her friends had discussed during the limo ride to their hotel the night before, her attention so focused on the excitement through the car windows.

"All right, ladies, I hereby make the Sin City Clique official." Juan, who could pass for a 50s pin-up girl with her low-cut, sleeveless dress if not for her multiple tattoos, raised her shot glass. A diamond stud in her cheek glinted in the lights. "This is our weekend, girls. No judgments. No regrets. What happens over the next forty-eight hours stays between the five of us for eternity."

"I solemnly swear I'm up to no good." They all

laughed when Kristie quoted her favorite Harry Potter movie before lifting a Bloody Caesar. "This weekend, we're moving forward." She smiled, but it didn't quite reach her eyes anymore.

"This weekend we get to enjoy ourselves and *fuck* what anyone else thinks." Aimee held her white-wine spritzer aloft. Coming from a prominent political family, Aimee had spent her life being groomed as a proper wife to a senator. But, so far, she had managed to avoid the goal her mother had set for her.

Sky's organic Fuzzy Navel rose to the rest of them. Thanks to a large gallery that had commissioned some of her pottery, she almost hadn't made it on the trip, and the women had been relieved when she'd checked into the hotel. "This weekend, we're going to follow our heart's energy to happiness."

Audrey toasted her friends with a rum and diet Coke. "This weekend, we celebrate our friendship since finding each other and bonding in the fiery forge of middle school. I don't want to think what my life would have been like without you."

Middle school had been a never-ending nightmare for her. Taunted for her weight, acne, and thick eyeglasses, Audrey might have stayed in the back corner of the classroom and faded into nothingness if not for the four women standing with her. They'd ended up on the same school bus to and from that pit of despair, discovered a friendship that had stood the test of time.

Clinking glasses, they cheered.

Still feeling a bit in awe of their surroundings, Audrey contemplated the lavish accommodations of the Castillo Resort and Hotel. They'd been treated like queens from the moment of their arrival the previous night, with mimosas by the pool that morning and then an afternoon of catching up over manicures and pedicures. They each had a date set up for that evening through the mysterious Madame Eve and her 1Night Stand dating service. But Audrey's anxiety had steadily risen as the day went on. She hoped she'd be attracted to the men who would be her date that evening. A wave of heat climbed up her neck, prickling her skin when she thought about what she'd requested. She set the glass down and pressed chilled fingers against her skin.

"Damn, Audrey, you're blushing enough to glow in the dark." Kristie laughed.

Audrey stuck her tongue out then reclaimed the cocktail and chugged it for courage. She took a deep breath to try to calm her racing nerves and the Vneck of her silk top shifted sideways. *My boobs are going to pop out of this top any second.* Tugging at the neckline, she attempted to gain more coverage.

"You're messing with perfection." Joan batted away Audrey's hands and straightened the material herself, dragging it down low enough that the edge of her lace bra almost peeked out. "You have a gorgeous rack, honey. It's time you stopped hiding it under men's sweaters and scarves. Pull your shoulders back and be proud."

Audrey had always been envious of Joan's self-confidence and *fuck 'em* attitude. All of her friends were much curvier than the fashion magazines said they should be, but Audrey was the heaviest of them all. She'd never been comfortable in her skin. Years of being called tubby and fatty still rang in her ears every time she saw her reflection. Even as an adult, after her skin cleared and recent laser eye surgery to get rid of her glasses, Audrey still had the insulting names embedded in her memory.

"What if they pop out in the middle of a conversation?"

"Oh, please. Your dates will be too busy drooling to be offended. And if it does happen, they'd better thank you." Aimee grinned and wrapped an arm around Sky's shoulders.

"You have the condoms I gave you, right?" Sky wiggled her eyebrows. Earlier, Audrey had found two dozen condoms tucked into her purse along with a small bottle of lube.

"She's blushing again. I guess she found the lube, too." Both Aimee and Sky started giggling and clinked their glasses together.

Audrey took another sip of her drink before saying anything. *Since when did they become mother hens?* "They're going to take one look at me and turn and run the other way."

"Hey, no talking like that." Joan frowned. "You're gorgeous, and we all want you to have the time of your fucking life this weekend."

"Don't think we haven't noticed how you tend to take care of the rest of us." Kristie gave her a hug. "This weekend we want you to do what makes you happy. This is Sin City, baby. What happens here stays here, so let's get crazy!"

***

Max Quinn lifted the corner of his cards and glanced at them before carefully counting out five, twenty thousand-dollar chips and pushed them toward the middle of the table. Three of the four other players threw their cards down and muttered select curse words. Nothing they did changed Max's poker face. Not the five hundred fifty thousand-dollar pot in front of him or the possibility he might lose it all. He'd spent years crafting the expression, and the only emotion Max would allow the arrogant man remaining across the table from him to observe.

The dark glasses Max wore also stopped his opponent from spotting him glance at his watch. He had fifteen minutes to finish the game before he was due at the hotel bar. His best friend and lover, Geoff, had arranged for them to meet their mystery date there. An excellent consolation, since Max would still have a good night even if he lost all his money on this flop.

It wasn't that he and Geoff couldn't get dates, but not all women liked to be shared with another man, and Max had a healthy appetite for both sexes. They were known around the high-rolling tables, and when they were on a roll, women fell all over them, but vanished the moment the money did. The men had become jaded after being judged according to the amount of cash in their pockets. Even so, when Geoff had come to him with the idea of approaching a dating site, Max had blown him off until he'd taken a better look at it and traded emails with Madame Eve. He'd even tried to convince her to meet them for drinks, but she'd graciously rebuffed him.

"You're bluffing, Quinn." Max's final adversary pushed the last of his chips into the center of the table. "All in."

Max had been counting on his opponent's arrogance to force a mistake like that. Lifting the corner of his two cards again, he confirmed he held the eight and six of hearts. He'd almost busted a blood vessel when the flop had revealed a seven, nine, and ten of those pretty hearts. A suspicious man would've thought fate had been sending him a message.

"Valentine's Day came early for me," he replied. Turning his cards over, he tossed them on the flop. Cheers echoed from the few people standing around, covering the other player's curse.

"Aren't you a real joker?" Cooper, one of the players who'd folded, stood and extended his hand to shake Max's. There were no real hard feelings. They understood the odds and risks with their gambling lifestyle. Max flipped the dealer a thousand-dollar chip then nodded to the pit boss. He'd make certain Max's winnings were collected and deposited in his casino account.

"Thank you, Mr. Quinn." The dealer slid the single chip into his tip box and then flipped his palms up to show the cameras above he hadn't attempted to palm any more.

"Thank you, George. I appreciate your patience." Max hadn't been born with a silver spoon in his mouth. He'd started his poker career on the other side of the table, working the midnight shifts, dealing cards to rich, arrogant assholes.

His phone vibrated for the third time in as many minutes. *Are you done, yet? Hurry up. Throw the goddamn hand if you have to.*

Like he'd ever do that. Max replied to Geoff's text, *Done. On my way.*

Dinner's on you, then.

"You cheap bastard," Max grumbled as he made his way to the exit. Geoff and his parents had more money than God, thanks to a trust fund from his grandparents. But, unlike his parents, Geoff refused to blow it all on an exorbitant lifestyle. He played smart and cautiously, not taking the risks Max often did with his money.

"Hi, Maxie." A gorgeous redhead stepped into his path. He stopped before trampling her, but not fast enough to prevent her ample breasts from getting smashed against his chest and giving him a clear view down the neckline of dress. "How 'bout you and I go get a drink?"

"Evening, Claudette." He laid his palms on her shoulders and gently eased her away. "I need to take a rain check, gorgeous. I'm late for a meeting with Geoff."

"Oh, why don't I come along?" She trailed her finger down his shirt, the blood-red nail clicking each button, traveling closer to his belt. "It's been a long time since I wiggled my way under the sheets with you two."

"It's a business meeting. No fun allowed."

Claudette stuck out her bottom lip and pouted. "But I could make it fun."

"I'm sure you would. Maybe another time, okay?" Max took a step back, widening the space between them. Whoever had coined the term *cougar* must have met Claudette first. She believed if a man ran, he wanted to be chased. The pot Max had won had caught her, nothing to do with him or Geoff personally.

"All right, but I'm holding you to that."

Max's cell phone chimed in his pocket. "That's going to be Geoff, wondering where I am. Have a good night."

"It would be better with you." Her lower lip pushed out again, and she looked at him from under her eyelashes. Max winked and blew her a kiss and hightailed it before another gold-digger managed to waylay him. He didn't doubt Claudette would set her sights on and dig her claws into another man with a big bank account before Max had made it out of the building.

***

Geoff Etherington dropped his cell phone next to his ice water. "Damn it, Max."

He'd been texting the hell out of his best friend and lover, but Max had a habit of losing track of time during a game and could easily be convinced to join another. All because of some crazy need to equalize their bank accounts. Geoff had bought a house and relocated to Vegas shortly after meeting Max. What had started as a fun weekend in Vegas with the other man had turned into a lifestyle change. Geoff had been living recklessly, with no ambition to do anything other than be like his parents. Meeting Max had forced him to change his self-absorbed view of the world. Geoff had spent the last year trying to convince his lover to move in with him. Supporting both of them wouldn't dent his bank balance, but Max had been determined to prove he could make it on his own first.

Geoff checked his watch for the hundredth time. Their date was due to arrive in fifteen minutes, although he figured that meant she'd be there in a half hour. It wouldn't be the first time a date had been *fashionably* late, a habit he detested but figured he had no control over.

When his phone vibrated, he snatched it up, afraid to read the message. It could be Max calling off because he'd gotten caught up in another game, or their date bailing on them for some equally stupid reason.

Keep your pants on for another five minutes, and I'll let you fuck me while she watches.

"Christ." Geoff took a large swallow of his water then crunched ice. His cock twitched at the possibility of some fun that night. But Max in a fetish mood had him thinking of a trip to the bathroom. Another quick check at the time assured him he had at least ten minutes before Max arrived and twenty-five before their date showed up. More than enough time for him to duck into a stall for a little self-pleasure to take the edge off. He slid off the stool to head toward the restroom.

He hadn't taken a single step before a bodacious female silhouetted in the entrance caught his attention. She rocked magnificent curves that had him wishing Max had arrived in time to see her. Ample breasts like hers weren't natural without an ass to match, and when she turned to skirt past a large group of people, he confirmed she had both in spades, along with a small waist. She swayed like Jessica Rabbit when she walked, and, suddenly, rubbing one off in a bathroom stall didn't hold any interest for him. He wanted this goddess at his feet, sucking him off as Max fucked him.

Men like them lived in a world of artificial women, both physically and emotionally, but this woman...her body moved like a natural-born seductress, yet reading her was like reading an open book. She yanked the neckline of her dress twice while he watched her. He'd bet she usually dressed more conservatively.

Just my luck. She's probably playing games with her husband in an attempt to spice up their marriage.

She scanned the patrons as though searching for someone and took her time looking him over. But his face hadn't caught her attention—the seductress stared at the rainbow on to his collar—the pin he'd mentioned he'd be wearing in an email to Madame Eve.

Son of a bitch. Jessica Rabbit is here for us.

After discreetly adjusting his raging erection, he gulped down his ice water. It would be a hell of a first impression if he tried to approach her with a hard-on tenting his dress pants. She'd probably haul off and deck him as a pervert. Not that he'd blame her.

Audrey wished she'd had a couple more drinks before venturing out to meet her dates. The dress Joan had insisted she wear had her nervous as hell. Her hands shook like a crooked accountant's in front of an auditor. She couldn't decide how to stand, was certain everyone she passed stared, and she couldn't be certain what they were thinking. That, in turn, sent her insecurities through the roof. Her boobs strained the neckline, threatening to pop out at any moment, and they jiggled when she walked in the high heels. What had started as an exciting adventure a couple of weeks earlier had evolved into something more terrifying than titillating.

What was I thinking, agreeing to this?

Quite a few men glanced her way when she entered the bar, her fingers clamped on her wallet to prevent tugging on her dress again. Some of patrons gave her the dismissive glance she'd been expecting, but others fixated on her chest long enough, she had to glance down to verify she hadn't suffered a wardrobe malfunction.

Madame Eve had explained one of her dates would be wearing a small rainbow pin on his shirt, but, so far, Audrey hadn't noticed anyone wearing one. Her gaze landed on a gorgeous man standing across the room. Short, dark-blond hair, sun-bleached at the tips, a bit of a scruffy beard, and the most incredible blue eyes. And he had to be at least six feet tall. He was way out of her league.

She glanced away, but a small, colorful glint grabbed her attention, and she almost stumbled onto her ass. *Mr. Out of My League* had a rainbow pin on his collar. When he turned away from her, she pretended not to notice. Evidently, he'd taken one look at her and changed his mind. Well, she did have some pride and refused to let him trample it. Heading straight to a barstool, but far enough away that he wouldn't think she'd been searching for him, she sat.

The bartender set a napkin in front of her. "Well, hello, gorgeous. What can I get you?"

Audrey ignored the compliment. They had to say such things to pad their tips. If she hadn't disgusted her alleged date so much, she might pretend to believe the guy told the truth. "Double rum and diet, please."

Less than a minute later, he delivered her drink with a wink. She smiled a thank-you and slid a bill across countertop. A large hand reached over and covered hers, trapping the bill.

"Put it on my tab, please. And I'll have another ice water."

A shiver of awareness shimmied over Audrey's bare shoulders at the voice next to her ear. She quickly pulled her fingers out from under his. His turquoise-blue eyes were only a few inches away from hers and her voice caught in her throat. Her heart fluttered wildly. She'd only ever seen that shade of blue in a picture of the sea in Greece.

"That's kind, but I can pay for my own drinks."

"I insist. It's the least I can do for my date."

The reminder of his reaction splashed on her ego like a bucket of ice water. "Listen...about that. You don't have to stick around, I'm sure you have plans that slipped your mind or something." Lifting her glass, she toasted him before turning her gaze to the bottles that lined glass shelves across from her. "No hard feelings. Thanks for the drink."

"You're turning me down already? We haven't had chance to talk yet."

The honest surprise in his voice caught her. His eyebrows had lifted, and he'd leaned away a few inches. His obvious shock echoed the tone of his words.

"No, I'm giving *you* an out." Audrey refused to play stupid games with him and didn't want to ruin her night any further by letting him trash her with sarcasm.

The bartender set a tall glass of water in front of him. "If he takes your *out*, gorgeous, I'm off in thirty minutes. I'd love to go to dinner with you."

She stared at the man and then at her date. They eyed each other like two wolves over a bunny. *A pudgy bunny, maybe.*

"Thank you, but I have other plans," she said before refocusing on the man beside her.

The bartender shrugged his broad shoulders and wandered off, no doubt to romance his way into a larger tip from someone else.

"Geoff Etherington." Her date held out his hand, and she took it. "I'm not sure why you think I need an *out*, but I have no interest in taking it."

A small, nervous kernel of hope puffed a bit in her chest. "Audrey Leport."

"My friend, Max, is on his way. The poker tournament he entered today went later than he'd expected." Geoff twisted the edge of her stool, turning her toward him. "This will get him moving quicker." He held up his phone. "Smile."

A cold wave of panic hit her in the chest. Putting on a brave face, she smiled but couldn't shake the sense of impending humiliation. "You warning him off?"

Typing on his phone, he paused and gave her a quizzical look. "That's twice you've done that."

"Done what?"

"Put yourself down and assumed you're not exactly what we asked for."

Audrey shrugged, but heat crept up her neck, and

her skin tingled. Was that what she'd been doing? "I don't know what you're talking about."

"Really? My mistake then." He finished typing then placed his phone next to her purse.

Resting his foot on the bottom rung of her stool, he braced his elbow on the bar, effectively trapping her with his body. She could escape but couldn't deny the thrill that came with having someone's complete focus. He hadn't turned tail and run like she'd expected, and seemed genuinely interested in her.

"What do you do, Audrey?"

"Nothing exciting...data entry for an accounting firm." She wanted to believe her physical appearance hadn't disappointed him, but her history tainted that hope. She'd promised herself she wouldn't allow anyone to make her feel insecure, and decided to address the elephant between them. "Let me ask you something—why 1Night Stand? I can't see you having a problem getting a date."

Geoff's eyebrows twitched as if the question took him by surprise. "Ah, but that's the interesting part; it's not just me. Max and I are a package deal, and most women don't like to share. What about you? What is it about sharing that you like?"

She shrugged and took a healthy swallow of her

drink. "I never have. It's kind of a fantasy of ours."

"Ours?" Winking, he slid her drink to the side, replacing it with his glass of ice water.

Warmth flooded her system. She'd never had anyone take care of her before, but his actions gave her pause. Was he genuinely interested in her sobriety or being a high-handed ass? "My friends and I...we all have similar fantasies regarding—" She waved her hand. "You know."

Geoff leaned closer, a mischievous grin on his beautiful lips. "What if I said I don't know? Would you tell me?"

Having his voice next to her ear in a near-whisper, caressing her skin, teased her senses into wanting more. The two drinks she'd consumed earlier with her friends and the half of a third cocktail had started to affect her. How could she put into words how the idea of being with two men, who happened to be lovers, made every hormone in her body want to jump up and dirty dance?

Uneasy, Audrey reached for her drink but Geoff slid it farther away from her and tapped the ice water in front of her. "Clear heads have more fun."

"Drunken ones aren't as self-conscious." She downed half the glass, hoping it blocked her hot cheeks from his view. If Aimee hadn't spent a half hour doing her makeup, Audrey would've pressed the cold glass against her cheeks.

"You have nothing to be self-conscious about, Audrey. You're stunning." His phone vibrated, but he didn't immediately grab it. His gaze never left her face. "You don't believe me, do you?"

"I have no reason to believe or disbelieve you."

The deep timbre of his laugh sent her stomach into crazy flip-flops. Geoff had a low voice, and his laughter vibrated through her, arrowing straight for her pussy. There was nothing mocking about it. In fact, if erotic had a sound, she imagined that's what it would sound like.

"You sure you're not in politics?" He glanced at his cell. With a smug and sexy smile, he passed it to her. "I want you to read what's there and let the words circle around in your head for a while."

Audrey read the thread of texts, her attention glued to the sentence at the top of the screen. *Keep your pants on for another five minutes, and I'll let you fuck me while she watches.*

A comment like that had her heart skipping a beat again before hammering back into a normal rhythm. Her dates couldn't know how badly she wanted exactly that, except she hoped to be an active participant instead of an observer. The picture Geoff had taken accompanied the message, and under it, he'd typed. *Audrey, our date....*

She reread Max's responses three times.

Exquisite

Don't start without me

2 min

I'm running

Chapter Two

Max tripped and almost tumbled face-first into a decorative fountain after Geoff texted him the picture of Audrey. He tapped it to expand the small image, and the same excited rush he'd experienced at the sight of his first centerfold filled him. Both he and Geoff made a living reading people. Hell, at times he'd had hundreds of thousands of dollars riding on his skill. And he could see Audrey had hips and full breasts and the potential for an amazing ass.

Damn it, I should have thrown the last cards. Fuck the money. Suddenly, his date had taken on an entirely new sense of urgency and instead of showing up late, he wished he'd been there when she'd arrived.

With the curves she'd been blessed with, he'd bet a thousand she'd been conditioned to think her body was less than desirable. Her forced smile and the placement of her arms blocking most of her chest confirmed it. The old adage that a picture is worth a thousand words couldn't be more accurate—this picture might as well been a novel about the woman they were to meet tonight. In Max's opinion, she was worth much more than the five hundred thousand he'd just won.

Texting Geoff back and forth on the way to meet them distracted Max. He lost his focus, and, after getting stuck behind a monstrous group of tourists, he almost lost his patience. After another quick text alerting Geoff of his ETA, he artfully dodged the zombie-speed, Vegas-struck crowd and started to jog, a plan forming. He'd been half-joking when he'd said earlier he'd let Geoff fuck him in front of her. What he really wanted was her under him at the same time, cradled between her thighs as his best friend pounded his ass. Sounded like the perfect end to their evening.

It didn't take more than a quick scan to spot the two of them. She perched on the edge of her stool while Geoff leaned close, invading her personal space. *Has he tasted her yet?* He and Max tended to be somewhat aggressive when attracted to someone, precisely how they'd met in the first place. Geoff had bumped into him in a bar, and the second Max saw his incredible blue eyes, he'd pinned him to the closest flat surface, desperate to taste him.

They'd fucked like bunnies in a coat room ten minutes later and had been together ever since. The memory had Max subtly adjusting the angle of his thickening cock. He and Geoff had been together for a little over two years, and, after a few scotch-fueled conversations in recent months, they'd agreed they wanted a woman in their lives, too. She'd have to be perfect, but when Geoff had come up with the idea of contacting a dating service, even one as exclusive as 1Night Stand, Max hadn't hesitated to voice his skepticism. Then again, if he never took chances, he wouldn't have reached the level of success he'd managed.

Madame Eve had been very through in her questions regarding their relationship and what they both wanted in the future. At the time, Max had thought her questionnaire far too in-depth for a single night of fun. Now, he understood what the mysterious woman had been thinking. Their possible future with a woman rested on Madame Eve's thoroughness.

Geoff glanced over Audrey's head and winked at him. "It's about time you got here."

Max cupped Geoff's jaw and kissed him before he said another word. The hunger in the kiss scorched him to his soul. Their mouths tangled as they fought for supremacy before Geoff bent to Max's will. Audrey might be their date, but he loved Geoff, and if that bothered her, Max wanted to know right away. She needed to be okay with their public displays of affection...to start. Other public displays could be discussed later that evening.

"Thanks for not leaving for dinner without me," Max said. "I ran."

"With greetings like that, you can be late any time."

Max lifted her hand and brushed his lips across her knuckles. "Hello, Audrey, I'm Max." A fine tremor ran up her arm, and her pulse fluttered at the base of her neck. "I hope I didn't embarrass you."

"Embarrassed is not a word I would use." Her cheeks were flushed; the pretty pink stained her neck and traveled to the rise of her beautiful breasts.

"Tell me what word bests describe how you're feeling."

"Ah, well." Audrey swallowed, her skin pinkening

further. "I'll need another drink before I answer that."

He decided not to push the issue right then. In fact, he wanted to get to dinner and start what promised to be a very delectable evening. "Do you mind if I grab a quick bite to eat at the restaurant before we go out?" The Castillo Resort had a number of excellent restaurants, and he hadn't eaten since lunch.

"Too bad we don't have coats." Geoff met his gaze while helping her slip off the stool. The hunger in his eyes reflected Max's desire.

Max nodded. "Truer words were never spoken."

"Why would you want a coat?" Audrey asked, glancing between them.

Max wrapped his arm around her waist, bringing her close. "Because, ten minutes after I met Geoff, I had him naked in a coat room hollering my name. It was the smartest decision I ever made, and damn if I'm not thinking of repeating it."

"You could have been caught." Her breasts tempted him with each breath she took, though she wore much more arousal than fear on her face.

Geoff bent his head near her ear without breaking the heated gaze his shared with Max. "That's half the fun. Max likes to fuck in public. He's a complete exhibitionist."

"Oh." She blinked like an owl—a very cute owl—her mouth in an O that had Max thinking about what he wanted to slip in there.

"It's true. I'd happily let Geoff drop to his knees right here and give me a blowjob while I stripped you naked, laid you out on the bar, and licked your pussy till you screamed."

She started shaking her head before he finished his sentence. "No way, not a chance. I don't get naked in public. Hell, I break out in hives at the thought of wearing a bathing suit outside of a changing room."

Max detested the way women allowed their confidence and self-worth be manipulated by marketing departments whose only goal was to make money. He'd be more than happy to show her how hard she could make him. "Challenge accepted."

"No, that's not, I don't...."

He ignored her sputtering as she tried to deny the challenge that he could get her naked in public. He didn't need to ask where her self-consciousness came from, nor did he care. Right then, all he cared about was what he could do to repair the damage to her self-image.

The crowd had expanded to the point they had to walk single file to leave.

"We have reservations in The Conservatory," Max said over his shoulder, and Geoff mentally pumped his fist. There couldn't be a more perfect place for them to start their night.

"That sounds lovely. Is it nearby?" Audrey clutched her purse tight enough he wondered if she's leave fingerprints in the leather. He found her nervousness endearing. *Could she be any more perfect?*

"Yes, it's part of this hotel," Max replied. He'd called in a big favor or three. The elite restaurant specialized in discretion, making it very popular with a certain A-list crowd.

Geoff dropped his attention to Audrey's ass swaying so perfectly in front of him. The temptation to grab ahold of her bodacious behind proved more tempting than he could resist. Avoiding someone barging past her, she stopped fast enough he closed the space and caressed her silk-covered ass. She gasped but didn't jump away. Instead, she glanced back at him, wide-eyed and blushing.

"Max isn't the only exhibitionist, is he?" Her

cheeks were still flushed, but some of the nervousness in her expression earlier had disappeared.

"No, ma'am. Given the right circumstances, Max is practically a prude compared to me."

She tugged on Max's wrist, and he halted, turning to crowd her much as Geoff had done a few minutes ago.

"Are you still thinking about her up on the bar?" Max asked. He rested his hands on her ribcage, just below her breasts.

She blinked a few times, and Geoff spotted the mixture of fear and curiosity warring behind her eyes. When Max caressed the underside of her breast with his thumb, she jumped, and the cutest squeak escaped her.

Geoff continued to run his fingers over her ass and pressed them gently at the apex of her thighs. "If I drop to my knees right now and push your dress up, are you going to be wet for me?"

Audrey gave her lips a quick swipe with her tongue. A myriad of expressions morphed across her face, but when her mouth opened, nothing came out. She glanced around, but neither he nor Max cared who might be watching them. Her fear and uncertainty finally stopped him from pushing her further. He refused to force her to do anything she didn't want, but he and Max had been very open in their communications with Madame Eve regarding their exhibitionist kink. She'd matched Audrey up with them, which meant she must be interested in that facet of their lifestyle as well.

"Okay, you two." Max shoved a hand through his long, dark hair. "You're making me horny as fuck, but I'm starving, too. Pick what we're going to do."

Geoff smiled down at Audrey. "Both."

"What do you mean?" Her eyebrows furrowed in confusion.

"You'll see." He pressed a palm on her lower back, and Max cocked out his elbow for her. When she laid her fingers on his arm, he trapped them with his and led them out of the bar.

Once they left, it was easier to stroll next to each other. Copying Max's gallant move, Geoff held out his own arm, and Audrey took it. He could get used to this. And once the shock of their teasing wore off, Audrey had regained her ability to speak and had a great sense of humor, although, when they tried to get more personal information out of her, she kept her cards close to her chest. Not that he blamed her—

Geoff had never felt such a deep attraction to a woman before, and part of him desperately wanted to know everything about her. He wanted to share everything he could with her as well, especially his and Max's project, something they never discussed with anyone.

"This is magical." Audrey looked around the restaurant.

Geoff totally agreed, taking in the restaurant's sumptuous décor. There were large crape myrtles in huge planters around the room, their blossoms creating a canopy overhead, interspersed with small twinkle lights. They looked incredibly real, but had to be replicas. He'd had the same trees in his yard growing up, and they'd made a hell of a mess."

The tables, covered in pristine white linen, were surrounded by luxurious, high-backed leather couches that curved around the tables. When Max gave him a seductive wink, Geoff didn't doubt they would be doing more than eating there.

"I wish I could fuck you on one of the tables in this place," Max growled at him. He closed the distance behind them and discreetly caressed Geoff's ass.

While Geoff was a big advocate of acting out their fantasies, there were places where they could get away with that and The Conservatory wasn't one of them. But pretending they could ravish each other at any moment added to the anticipation. He wasn't about to tell Audrey that and ruin the fun. He'd been hard ever since she'd sashayed into the bar, and he welcomed the additional illicit kick to his arousal.

"By the end of dinner, I want all three of us hot and ready to fuck," Max said. "We're going to the club after this."

The maître d' escorted them to a table near one wall, preventing Geoff from replying. Audrey clutched her purse like a lifeline again, her gaze darting around the room. Fortunately, the trio wouldn't be on display in the middle of the room, but a large fireplace next to them would draw some attention, perfect for teasing Audrey.

Geoff ushered her into the center of the booth, between them. While he wanted to be able to tease Max as well, there would be lots of time for that later. The purpose of their evening was to decide if they truly wanted to take this path by including a woman in their lives. There were no guarantees in life and Audrey might happily go back to hers the next day. Yet, the thought of her leaving them behind didn't sit well Geoff already.

No sooner had they placed their orders and been given some privacy than she said to Max, "What club?"

He leaned over and whispered in her ear. Geoff lifted his water to hide his smile when her jaw dropped. He could almost make out her blush in the subdued lighting. Her honest reactions were refreshing, though she was jaded enough not to fall for every line. Many women in Las Vegas had honed the ability to create illusions that hid their true feelings and intentions, but not Audrey.

"Is he making you nervous, Audrey?" Geoff trailed his fingers along her arm, enjoying the goose bumps that rose. He loved a woman sensitive to touch.

"I'd be lying if I said no."

"And you don't lie often, do you?" Max caressed a few wayward strands of hair before running his lips along the tense muscle in her neck.

"No." She puffed out the answer on a quick breath, her eyes glazed, and Geoff wondered if she was imagining what they wanted to do to her.

"No, of course you don't. You're a good girl, aren't you?" He took her wrists and brought them around to the small of her back. "I want you to keep your hands here for a little bit, let us play with you. If you're willing, after dinner, we'll take it a bit further."

Later, you can sit on my lap and let Geoff lick your pussy and my cock at the same time. Then, just as you're about to come, I want to bend you over and fuck you while you suck Geoff off.

The words Max had whispered in her ear when they'd first sat fluttered in Audrey's thoughts as he continued the seductive banter. She hadn't really been paying attention to their conversation until he'd said the words and Geoff had wrapped his fingers around her wrists, holding tight, forcing her breasts out even farther. There would be a wardrobe malfunction of epic proportions if she didn't watch how she moved.

Not having the best posture, she tended to hunch to hide her large breasts—when not trying to hide her ass, or hips, or the hundred other parts of her body she didn't like. Sitting with her arms behind her prevented her from slouching.

"You are absolutely magnificent," Max said along the sensitive skin below her ear.

Her nipples hardened. Even her bra padding couldn't hide them. She glanced over at the other tables in the room, but no one seemed to be paying any attention to them. *Thank God.*

"Someone's going to see us," she murmured. Clenching her fingers, Audrey fought the urge to move them out from under Geoff's and fall into her old habit of dropping her shoulders forward. His warm grasp remained on her wrists.

"That's the plan, beautiful." Max's breath was a hot caress against her ear. "We like playing in public, and I want to get at least one orgasm out of you before dinner is through."

At his casual arrogance, her stomach flipped. This was the part where she'd fail to live up to their expectations. "I'm not that sensitive, but it's okay. I can still have fun without coming. Why don't you let me play with you?"

Both men straightened and stared at her like she'd completely lost her mind.

"Unacceptable." Max ran a hand through her hair then gripped a handful. Little pinpricks danced along her scalp, nothing painful, more of a reminder who had control.

Geoff squeezed her wrists for a split second before relaxing then ran his tongue along her collarbone and kissed the hollow at the base of her neck. Her arms broke out in goose bumps again.

"You don't want me to?" The situation confused her. Her ex had never turned down an offer from her, especially if it meant he didn't have to reciprocate.

"Hell, yes, but we already know what we like." Max nuzzled her ear. "We want to know what turns *you* on."

"I have a feeling you're not going to tell us, darlin'. Or is it that you've never had a lover take his time and find out?" Geoff pulled one of her hands out from behind her then, in a low voice, said, "Keep the other one there."

"I guess, not really. I know what I like to do to myself."

Max groaned stroked her inner thigh, teasing the sensitive skin under the hem of her dress, while Geoff pressed his lips on her palm. "That's a sight I hope you're kind enough to treat us to."

"I'll show you, if you show me."

The waiter returned with their drinks. Without making eye contact, he poured glasses of champagne then placed the bottle in a silver chiller on the table.

Max caressed the skin much higher on her leg. He didn't touch her pussy, but his intentions were clear, and she grew wet in response.

Geoff instructed the waiter, "We'll have the Trio."

"Yes, sir." The server backed away and left them alone.

There was something very illicit about sitting while two men fondled her in front of a stranger. Audrey had almost wanted the waiter to meet her gaze so she could determine if he knew what they were doing.

After he'd departed, Max and Geoff eased away, and she immediately missed them. The promise of a climax while being restrained in the middle of a restaurant had her pussy throbbing with each heartbeat. Max handed her the champagne flute before taking a sip of his own.

"What are you two playing at?" she asked. Irritation and insecurity started to harshen her mood. Were they toying with her emotions? Had they changed their minds?

"Pacing ourselves, Audrey. We don't want to overwhelm you and have you take off on us before dessert gets here." Geoff continued to drink water, his champagne left untouched.

"Are you sure?"

Max cupped her chin and turned her face toward him. "I think I know what's going through your head right now, but let's put a stop to that immediately.

Both Geoff and I appreciate a woman who looks and feels like a woman should. If we wanted some stick-thin, artificial cougar...well, they're a dime a dozen around here.""

"Neither are we interested in adding a twink to our family," Geoff agreed. "We want a woman with luscious tits and an ass we can hold onto when we're fucking. You, Audrey, are perfect."

In a few short minutes, they had managed to crush her insecurities and completely turn her on. She lifted her glass and tasted the perfectly chilled bubbly, the effervescence dancing on her tongue. Without being too obvious, she shifted in her seat and attempted to ease the dull, sensual throbbing in her core. The men seemed to have a sixth sense about her, and, from their grins, she wondered if they also read minds.

"What's most important is how you feel." Geoff caught the hem of her dress and slowly slid it up her legs until it bunched at the top of her thighs. He teased the edge of her panties. "How would you feel if I got rid of these?"

She kept her legs closed, feeling a bit on display, but so incredibly turned on. "To be honest, I'm not entirely certain."

Max rested an arm across the back of the bench, behind her. "Let's take them off with the promise that, if you ask for them, I'll return them to you."

Audrey gnawed at her lower lip as she tried to decide. *It's so tempting.* To take the chance and experience a delicious fantasy. But the fear of change that had kept her in a dead-end job for years still tempered her decisions. Finally, she asked, "You promise?""

"I swear it. I know it's early to ask you to trust us, but you can." Max hooked a finger in the silk covering the hip closest to him. "All you have to do is lift up enough for us to slide these off you."

Taking a deep breath, she rose a smidge. Max and Geoff moved quickly, sliding her underwear off and lifting her dress out from under her so when she sat down, her butt landed on cool leather. Max brought the silk to his nose and sniffed.

Embarrassment surged through her, and she yanked his arm down. "Don't do that!"

"Please don't tell me some idiot made you feel self-conscious about your body's natural scent." Geoff caressed her thigh, so close to her pussy she clenched her legs together again. "We're not silly boys who don't appreciate every beautiful nuance of the female body, and that includes smell and taste." The last couple words were said against her neck, sending shivers along her arms.

Glancing at Max, who'd thankfully lowered her panties, she remembered they were in a restaurant with people nearby. Surprise warmed Audrey's cheeks as one of two women sitting at a table a few feet away winked at her.

"I forgot what we're doing can be seen." Desire for more warred with the desire to put her clothes back on properly.

"Ignore them. They're just envious. You're an incredible woman. All they can do is watch and wish they were us."

"Don't you mean they wish they were me?" She'd be lying if she believed everything the men said to her.

Max moved forward and tucked her panties into her empty palm before twining his fingers with hers. Geoff captured her other hand in his and kissed her knuckles.

"No, we have it right." He lightly stroked her collarbone and then along the swell of her breasts. "Now that you're all bare under your dress, why don't you spread your legs for me?"

Her chest froze at the thought of exposing herself. Driven by a need she couldn't name, she wiggled her ass. Warm juices coated her pussy. Had she made a mess of the seat beneath her? Just the idea of letting them touch her right then created an inner battle. She darted a quick glance at the nearby table, but the woman had returned to her conversation and didn't appear to be paying them any mind.

"You'll get us kicked out of here," she said.

"Nice try." Max gently slipped his hand between her legs and encouraged her to spread them. "You wear every thought on your face like a beacon."

Geoff began to stroke her, teasing her. She was so damned wet, there wasn't any resistance when he parted her sensitive pussy lips and stroked between them.

"That's our girl," he said. "We're not going to do anything to embarrass you, but we like to keep you on edge." Her juices coated his skin, and she couldn't tear her gaze away when he raised two fingers to his mouth and sucked them. "You taste incredible. I can't wait to lick your cream off Max's cock and enjoy the combined taste of you."

A tremor raced through her at the erotic mental picture created by his words.

"Fuck, that's a hot thought." Reaching across her lap, Max cupped the thick ridge outlined on the front of Geoff's pants. "You two are getting me hard enough to hammer nails."

"Really?" She'd never thought of herself as a seductress, or considered a man would get turned on by thinking about her.

Max, his eyes almost black in the dim lighting, led her palm to Geoff's groin. The thick length pulsed behind his fly. "Rub Geoff, too."

Her champagne flute rattled slightly when she set it on the tabletop. With the power back in her court, she ran her fingers down Geoff's rock-hard dick while mimicking the action on his partner.

Geoff assumed the same position as Max, leaning back with his arms outstretched. His partner playing with the hair at his nape. In turn, he stroked Max's cheek while they watched her manipulate their cocks through their pants.

Max groaned and stopped her. "Christ, you have no idea how badly I want to flip you up on this table and fuck you hard and fast."

"Let's go find the coat room, and we'll both fuck her," Geoff said, trapping her fingers against his bulging erection.

"Why don't you both undo your pants, and I can do this right?" The bold words came out of nowhere, but Audrey wouldn't take them back.

"Because we're not the ones are going to come first, darlin'," Geoff crooned as he topped her champagne again.

"We're getting to know what each of us likes before we get to the fun stuff." Max winked at her before reaching for the bread basket sitting on the other side of the table.

Unaware of the activity around them, Audrey hadn't noticed the couple at the nearby table had left. She'd been so focused on Max and Geoff, the entire world had disappeared.

Max buttered a piece of warm bread and passed it to her, but Audrey shook her head, unable to eat the carbohydrate treat with the copious amount of butter he'd smeared on it.

"You have to try this." He passed another piece over to Geoff. "The butter is sweetened with honey. I might just ask them to bag some up so I can lick it off you later."

"Why wait till later?" Geoff quipped before discreetly smearing the slice along the soft swell of her right breast..

The action both appalled and excited her. "You did not just do that."

"Better believe it. Now, take a bite of yours, or the next piece goes between your legs." Geoff grinned.

Max crowded closer to her. "Lift your chin, Audrey." Tempted to defy him, she wanted to see if Geoff would follow through with his threat.

"Do it, sweetheart." Geoff met her gaze as if reading her mind. "I have no qualms about licking your pussy in the middle of this restaurant."

It didn't matter that she might not know them all that well. There was no resisting their advances, and she didn't want it to end. After darting a quick look around to ensure no one was watching, she tipped her chin up, and Geoff chuckled.

"Coward," he crooned.

Max followed the buttery path over her skin with his mouth. The sensation of his hot breath on her breasts had her on the verge of begging for them to stop teasing her. Geoff must have noticed because, a moment later, he stroked her soaked pussy before circling her clit.

"You won't believe how wet she is, Max...."

She started to utter a denial, but Geoff claimed her mouth in a kiss that wordlessly demanded she concede to him, his tongue stroking hers in a long, sensual tease. She didn't want to resist a moment longer."

Another groan vibrated the skin of her neck when Max's fingers joined Geoff's, tangling on her clit. She'd never imagined the eroticism of two men touching her could be this good.

Someone pushed a digit into her pussy, and the unexpected intrusion had her breaking away with a gasp. Overwhelmed and turned on, she trembled. Clutching Geoff's thigh with one hand, she gripped the front of Max's shirt with the other. Geoff slipped his wet fingers between his lips, licking them clean. He looked around them and then nodded to Max.

Her vaginal walls fluttered and clenched as Max pumped in and out. "You're pussy is so wet, so tight. This is just the start. Come for us, Audrey."

The friction of his surging rhythm on her clit increased with each stroke. She tightened her hold on Geoff's thigh and quivered. The orgasm she'd been so sure couldn't happen crashed over her like a tidal wave. Clenching her teeth, she buried her face in Geoff's neck to prevent a scream, though a small part of her desired to let the entire restaurant know of the pleasure she'd received.

Max embraced her and murmured as Geoff stroked her hair. "Relax, baby. Max likes to cuddle."

Along with Max's steady heartbeat, a low rumble of amusement echoed under her ear. "Geoff's every bit the cuddler I am."

"I like this." The residual throb of her clit hummed through her body, and Audrey had no intention of moving anytime soon. Relaxing against each of them was the extent of her energy, although she'd have been happier to stretch out in a bed with them both.

Geoff and Max weren't the least bit put out by her lazy attitude. They fed her bites of dinner from the large platter their server delivered, while she relaxed. Having two gorgeous men feed her was a luxury she'd never experienced, especially decadent because they stole kisses between bites. Her banked arousal continued to smolder throughout their meal. They were obviously in love, and she wished that her time with them would last longer than one night. She never felt excluded or like a *third wheel* at any point.

"What is this club you're taking me to?" Audrey relaxed into Geoff's embrace. Her palm rested on Max's leg, her fingers entwined with theirs.

"A special place where we can indulge in some of

our favorite hobbies." Geoff's low voice brushed the sensitive edge of her ear.

Wanting a night to remember, she'd asked for something special and wild that she'd never be able to experience again. Bittersweet, in a way, since the more time she spent with them, the more she couldn't imagine ever feeling the same way with anyone else.

"Does that mean I can reciprocate some of the attention you've given me?"

He chuckled. "We're counting on it."

Chapter Three

udrey hadn't a clue what to expect when Geoff held open a large door for her and Max. There hadn't been any lineup or flashing lights around the entrance. Only a brass sign attached to the brick entrance that read, *Observation Inn ~Tueor Fornicatio~*.

Strange name. "I thought you said this was a club?"

"It's a very private club that takes the whole *What happens in Vegas* slogan to heart." Max's hand pressed against her lower back, warmth radiating through the fabric barrier. "But there are certain ironclad rules that will always be respected."

"What rules?"

"For starters, *no means no.*" Geoff followed them, removed Max's jacket from her shoulders, and gave it to a woman at a small coat check desk. "No exceptions."

Audrey looked around the entrance to the club. It had a masculine decor with dark-wood moldings and beige-stucco walls, and her heels sank into the plush carpet as she walked. The entire place screamed money in a quiet, classy way, without the obnoxious overabundance so typical in Las Vegas.

The woman gave her a small smile and nodded in greeting. "Good evening, ma'am, Mr. Etherington, Mr. Leporte. Your table is ready. If you require lodgings for the night, please don't hesitate to let me know, and I'll have your room prepared."

"Thank you, Angelica," Max said as they passed.

Linking arms with Audrey, they led her though another door, and she couldn't hold back her curiosity. "You have a room here? Do you do this often?" A green tinge of envy colored her mood, but she tried to tamp it down before it got the best of her. She refused to ruin her fantasy night with reality or misplaced jealously.

"All the members have the option of staying, but we rarely do. Max and I have an incredibly comfortable bed at home we prefer to sleep in."

When Geoff winked, Audrey wasn't sure if he meant he planned to have her experience their bed firsthand or simply teased her. They left the short hallway and entered the main area, the lights too dim for her to see his expression clearly.

The low lighting didn't hide the sight in front of her—a topless woman sitting on a barstool, making out with another woman who fondled her breasts. Audrey had never considered herself attracted to women, but she couldn't deny the fascination watching the beautiful display of passion. While some people casually observed them, not everyone focused on the pair, but Audrey couldn't tear her eyes away as the guys led her past a couple tables.

"Did we shock you already?"

She peered back at Geoff and shook her head. "No, I'd have to say they're much more arousing than shocking."

Max spun and cupped her face, planting a kiss on her mouth. Then the ridge of Geoff's erection pushed against the upper swell of her ass, daring her to sway her hips and tease him, which she did. Geoff rewarded her with a low groan and a sharp nip at the base of her neck. She'd been claimed, and he wanted everyone to know she belonged to the two of them, a fanciful dream she desperately wanted to believe could be possible.

"What do you think, Audrey? Does the idea of strangers watching Geoff and I take you turn you on?"

Insecurity raised its ugly head, demanding to know how she could possibly think of herself as good enough for them. *But, they're here with me...who cares what anyone else thinks.* All she managed was a gulp of air and a shake of her head.

"Thank God, because you have me so goddamned hot right now." Max carried the demeanor of a man used to getting whatever he wanted. "I'm tempted to toss you on the nearest table and fuck you both senseless."

Geoff wrapped an arm around her torso before reaching out to grab Max's long hair and pull him closer. "While that sounds incredible, I do recall you saying you'd let me fuck you while Audrey watches."

The mental picture slammed through her, and heat radiated through her pussy. She'd already had one orgasm. Fair play demanded the men have a chance to catch up. The possibility of watching them together was even more erotic then she'd ever imagined.

"I really like the idea of a private show."

"There won't be anything private about it." Geoff

gave Max a kiss that multiplied Audrey's desire by a hundred. "I think our date likes to play both sides of this kink, Max. Our own little exhibitionist and voyeur all rolled into one."

Max smiled down at her, his lips swollen. "Let's get this party started."

Grabbing her hand again, he led them to a padded, U-shaped bench in the middle of the room. The back was high enough to be comfortable but didn't offer much in the way of privacy. The middle section angled like a recliner, with small tables built into ends.

A pitcher of water and three glasses sat on one of the tables, but the large, artistic light, like a giant lotus tissue-paper flower, hanging over them caught her attention. Max tapped something on the side of the bench that turned it on, bathing the area in a soft light.

Audrey's insecurities flared again, causing her to question the entire idea. Playing with Max and Geoff at the restaurant and the threat of being caught had added to the intensity of the experience, but to literally be on display changed everything.

"Does the light have to be on?"

Geoff's large, warm body corralled her, and he

caressed her waist. "We want to show off for you. It turns me on so much to know you'll be watching us. The light merely lets everyone else know we're welcoming spectators." His voice reminded her of a little devil on her shoulder, tempting her. Except no angel sat on her other shoulder to talk her out of it. "This is our kink, sweetheart, and there is no law that says you have to join in, although we both would love it if you would. It's completely up to you. Trust me, if you want us to turn off the light and keep this amongst the three of us, that's okay, too." He moved to the soft music being played in the background, slowly grinding his erection along her tailbone and ass.

Audrey shook her head again. Nervous anticipation wracked her system, but she couldn't deny how hot and wet her pussy had become at the thought of not only observing, but perhaps participating. She pictured slipping to her knees and sucking on Max's cock as Geoff fucked him.

"I don't know what you're thinking, but the expression on your face is enough to make me fuck hard and fast." Max had flopped back against the recliner, arms spread out on the cushions lining the bench. "Come over here and let me play with you."

Geoff patted her ass then gave her a little push. "Go ahead. I want to get a couple of things before I wipe that smirk off his face."

Stepping closer to Max, she allowed him to draw her to his body. Glancing up at the light for a moment, she returned her gaze to him.

"Don't think about it too much," he said. "You don't have to do anything other than what you are comfortable with. This isn't a test, just a bit of fun." He pulled her down until she straddled his hips, encouraging her to sit in his lap. "If you aren't comfortable, we'll leave and find a nice, cozy bed to curl up in."

A weight lifted off her. There wouldn't be a chance of her ruining the night. She was curious and very aroused, but insecurity could be an evil little voice in her head. *What if Max and Geoff are offended by my soft shape when they get a good look at me?* Regardless, the idea of strangers seeing her naked shot a sharp jolt of arousal over her.

"Do you have any idea how beautiful you are?" Max skimmed her thighs then stroked her arms. "Your skin's like silk...." He brushed a thumb across her lower lip then the edge of her jaw before curling a hand around her nape. "Come here."

His fingers speared through her hair, and he tugged her near with a gentle, almost reverent touch. But the embers from earlier play returned to life with a heated blast, and dark hunger soon swamped them. He gripped her hair, controlling her movements while deepening their kiss.

Tracing her tongue with his, he might as well have created a direct line from her mouth to her clit. Each stroke pulsed along her nerves. She pulled at his shirt, fumbling with the buttons. Rocking her pelvis on his erection didn't bring her close enough to the relief she craved, but she couldn't help herself.

"Don't let him come, Audrey." Geoff's voice pierced the passionate veil that had fallen over her.

She'd been practically riding Max in the middle of a club where anyone could see. Max growled low, clutching her hips as she ground down on his cock. She pushed his shirt aside to expose his chest.

Tracing down the middle of his pecs to the well-defined stomach muscles, she said, "I think you made Geoff a promise, and I don't want you to welch on your deal."

"Woman, you are driving me insane." Max clenched his abs as she slowly undid the fastening of his trousers.

The dampness from her wet pussy on the fabric reminded her how ready she was. "I might have ruined your pants. I'm sorry."

"I'm not. Next time, I'm going to let you hump me till you come all over them."

Next time? Will we have a next time? This was supposed to be a one-night stand. Maybe he was only pretending there'd be more so things wouldn't feel too awkward later?

"Don't overthink it, Audrey. Let it happen." Geoff's voice nearby distracted her from the thoughts plaguing her. When she turned her head, she found his face right next to hers. He kissed her, tasting every bit as intoxicating as Max, who trailed a lick across her neck. The combination of their attentions revved her internal lust bunny into overdrive. Four hands, four lips, two hard cocks teasing her with erotic promises, seducing her.... She wanted something she hadn't believed possible.

"Okay, Max can wait," Geoff said. "I have to get this dress off you."

Audrey opened her eyes, blinking against the light. She and the men were literally on display, and insecurity sucker-punched her bravery. "Oh, no! I've heard that only the lowest of the low back out of deals. I don't want Max's reputation to be ruined."

"Oh, darlin', he nuked his reputation long ago; don't you worry about that." Humor sparkled in Geoff's gorgeous eyes.

"Hey, I'm right here."

She peered up through her lashes at Max. His face didn't give anything away , but she had a sneaking suspicious she hadn't fooled him with her excuse.

He narrowed his eyes. "I never welch."

After a quick kiss, Audrey sat alone on the reclining bench, vaguely aware of a few spectators pausing in the darkness beyond the light. Pushing the awareness out of mind, she focused on the gorgeous men in front of her, fascinated by the seductive way Geoff pushed the shirt off Max's shoulders and tossed it on the bench. Geoff's blond hair glimmered under the soft lighting, and he appeared almost angelic compared to Max.

"Turn around." Geoff's voice held a sharp edge, and Max immediately turned and faced her. His head dropped back on his shoulders as Geoff caressed his bare skin, slowly sliding down his torso to his waist. He hooked his thumbs in the sides of Max's pants and underwear and tugged them down his legs. His cock escaped its confines, stretching toward Audrey.

She wished she were braver. As Geoff stroked Max from root to tip, she wanted to join in but couldn't bring herself to do it under the spotlight. *I don't want to ruin this.*

"Step out of your pants and straddle Audrey's legs, Max, then bend over and grab the back of the cushions."

Max kept his gaze locked on hers while he loomed over her. "Touch me, Audrey, Please."

His body blocked the light, and the shadows embraced her, boosting her courage. She cupped his balls and stroked her palm around them and up the satin-wrapped marble of his cock, heat radiating from it. Geoff dropped to his knees behind him, and a moment later a low growl emanated from behind Max. A shudder rocked through him, and his cock bobbed under her palm, but the calm expression on his face never changed.

"Are you always this in control, Max? What's Geoff doing right now?" She wanted to hear the words, wondering if that would shake his control.

"He's rimming me." Max's eyes fluttered closed, and his head dropped, hiding his face. "Fuck, I love the feel of his tongue on my ass and your soft fingers around me. You're both making my head spin."

"We're just getting started, Maxie." Geoff snatched a condom off the end table, and she heard the slight metallic crinkle when he ripped it open.

"I think he's planning to do more than just tongue you." Audrey eased back into the recliner, her heart thudding at the knowledge of what they were going to do.

Geoff stood with a sensual grin and positioned himself behind Max. The moment he breached Max, they groaned in pleasure and started to rock against each other.

"Our Audrey is going to watch you, Max. Don't hide behind your mask. Show her what you're really feeling."

Almost immediately, the stoic calm expression she'd gotten used to melted away. A myriad of emotions, from pain to intense pleasure, played across Max's features, fascinating her. He braced his hands on either side of her shoulders, and she shifted in her seat, certain she must be sitting in a puddle of her own juices by then. The sight of Geoff nipping at Max's shoulders, knowing he claimed his body, was the most erotic image she'd ever seen. When Geoff bit down sharply on the crook of Max's neck, his cock twitched, and a creamy pearl decorated the rounded crown.

A low moan rumbled from his chest. "Fuck, yes, baby." Max's muscles twitched under his skin, from shoulders to waist, like a seductive dance. "I'm going to ruin your dress, Audrey." His dark eyes were black. "Pull down your dress and let me cover your breasts."

She'd never understood the eroticism behind a man ejaculating on her until that moment. She wanted to be an intricate part of them. Instead, she opted to be more intimate and said, "I can do one better. Geoff, can you support Max and step back a little bit?"

"With pleasure," Geoff slipped his arms around Max's chest and lifted him, allowing Audrey some room to slip to her knees in front of his legs.

"Fuck." The curse slipped past Max's clenched teeth. "You can't. I can't....won't last."

"Snowballs, snowbanks, Antarctica, popsicles—"

"Shut up, Geoff."

"Just trying to cool you down a bit, lover."

Audrey smiled at their banter while curling her tongue over the tip of Max's cock, collecting the cream. Another muttered curse from above encouraged her to give him something to swear about. She couldn't take his entire length but would take as much as possible.

"How do you like that, Max, we're both fucking you now?" Geoff asked.

"Not...helping."

She met Max's hungry black gaze. He watched her giving him head through heavy-lidded eyes. When his gaze flicked past her, she figured someone had to be watching them.

Challenge accepted. With that, her bravery cold-cocked her insecurity for good. The tip of Max's cock brushed the back of her throat, and she swallowed around the blunt crown.

"FuckyesGodJesusChrist!"

With one hand at the base of his cock, Audrey gripped Max's thigh with the other and took every hot, musky drop of cum coating her throat. Geoff's low snarl heralded his own completion and she gently let Max slip from her lips, kissing the tip. Geoff pushed him into the position he'd been in before, gripping the cushions on either side of her shoulders. He increased his speed until his head tipped back and he shouted toward the ceiling. Both he and Max collapsed on the cushions, but not before they scooped her up and ensconced her between them.

Tingles danced along Audrey's nerves, sparking

like a live wire. The two of them orgasming in front of her was the most arousing exhibition she'd ever witnessed. The shadows might have held strangers, but any concern their presence caused her paled in comparison to the deep, aching need pulsing in her core.

Geoff shifted away from her and discreetly disposed of the condom before returning to her. She didn't have time to contemplate her next move before Max slid his hand under her knee and lifted her leg. He reached between her them and adjusted something below the bench seat.

"Can you feel the ledge with your feet?"

Something he'd done had created a little step; when she rested her feet on it her knees were high enough to tilt her pelvis. Cool air waved over her exposed pussy, but a heartbeat later, Max trailed a warm finger through the slit.

"Geoff, feel her. She's wetter than I'd imagined."

When her legs began to snap shut, Geoff braced them open, stopping her. "Don't hide from us." His face blocked out everything around them as he closed the distance between them. His gorgeous eyes caught her focus, and the arousal reflected in them reassured her more than words could ever have.

Max played with her soaked pussy while she stared into the eyes of another man, stimulating her further. "Everything you think is right there on your face. Don't ever play poker." His infectious grin caused her to smile back. He swirled the pad of his thumb around her clit, enticing her closer to orgasm. Max used her natural lubrication to slip a finger inside, and the sudden invasion caught her off guard. Sexual heat bloomed through her.

"Look at me, Audrey." Geoff's voice sounded so far away, and she hadn't realized she'd closed her eyes. "Would you rest your feet on the step again for me?"

"God, you are so hot and wet." Max said. She rested her feet on the ledge, and he began to stroke in and out. Geoff joined him, his fingers playing with her pussy, paying close attention to her clit.

All she wanted to do was drop her head back and close her eyes and let the incredible pleasure wash over her, but the guys wanted her to watch them. It delayed her orgasm, frustrating her to no end.

Max paused. "You're used to racing to the end aren't you?"

He and Geoff took turns kissing her while she rolled her hips against his hand. Their touches were driving her mad, seducing her. But whenever she teetered on the edge of orgasm, they'd stop, and the pinnacle would drift away.

"I like to come. Since when did that become a bad thing?" *Shit, that sounded snippy.* But instead of being insulted, they laughed.

"Because, sometimes, denial makes everything more intense." Max eased the neck of her dress to the side, revealing her lavender-lace bra. He folded back the lace and exposed her nipples to the cool air.

Geoff bent his head at the same time as Max, and they twirled and licked her nipples. She clenched with need when their tongues stroked each other and one nipple in the same moment, as though they fought over a single red raspberry. Max continued to use his teeth and tongue, toying with her, while Geoff wrapped his lips around the other tip. He sucked and drew it deep.

She'd never recalled her breasts being that sensitive, but the combined ministrations pulled at a throbbing ache in her core. Their worship focused solely on her pleasure, drawing a current straight to her pussy like the frayed end of a live wire sparking with white heat.

Focusing on her breasts didn't prevent them from playing with her pussy, feeding her desperate, growing need. One of the men rubbed her clit enough to make her moan, but not near long enough to finish her off.

"Oh, please, do it again."

"Soon," one of them crooned.

Two fingers circled her entrance before plunging into her. Part of her brain wanted to holler about morality and appropriate behavior, but the lusty rush of pleasure demolished any apprehension she felt. They pushed into her at the same time, short-circuiting all thoughts. So far beyond what she'd ever expected, their movements disabled her ability to process anything but the desire igniting her body.

She arched. "Yes! Again. More." Her hips rocked in time with their rhythmic stroking.

"Christ, you're so damn hot," Geoff breathed.

Max grunted. "She's going to get hotter in a moment."

Audrey's body trembled as they kissed a path down her chest and stomach. Their lips tickled and stroked her body, nipping her skin, awakening erogenous zones she'd had no idea existed.

"Do you remember what I said to you, Audrey?" Max asked.

At the club, you can sit on my lap and let Geoff

lick your pussy and my cock at the same time. Then, just as you're about to come, I want to bend you over and fuck you while you suck Geoff off. Max's earlier words echoed until shivers raced over her body, and her nipples crinkled.

"Oh, yeah, she remembers."

Max grinned at Geoff's comment. Their woman was so fucking wet, he figured she'd drip if she stood. Not that he had any intention of letting her do that. His cock had jumped to life again the moment his and Geoff's fingers penetrated her. Finger-fucking her with the man he loved and watching her writhe beneath their touch created a special intimacy. Was it too soon to think that way about Audrey? *Maybe. But when has that stopped me?*

As Geoff kept her distracted and enthralled, Max reached for one of the condoms from the side table.

"I need to feel the tight pussy." He sat and encouraged her to straddle his lap while facing outward. The shadows shifting around them were evidence they'd drawn quite a crowd, but she seemed oblivious for the moment. As her voluptuous body moved over him, he lifted her dress and stroked her luscious ass. "Have I told you how perfect you are?"

Her cunt wrapped around his dick like molten gold as his tip penetrated her for the first time. Thanks to the mind-blowing orgasm he'd been treated to, he'd be good for a lengthy fuck. But that wasn't in the cards when her muscles clamped down on him, and each push gained him an inch but stole more of his control.

Easing her dress from her shoulders, she bared her breasts completely. *How can she be so self-conscious? She's breathtaking.* He hoped keeping her dress pooled at her waist would give her a sense of security. Geoff tapped the inside of his knees, and Max opened his legs at the silent request.

"Oh God." Audrey fell back on his chest, and Max cupped her breasts, pinching her tight nipples as her pussy rhythmically clenched around him. With her head tilted against his shoulder, he had a clear view down her body to the top of Geoff's head between her legs.

Watching Geoff tongue their lover took attraction to an entirely new level. The slick sheen on his mouth was like lip gloss, and Max's balls tightened. An image of Geoff and Audrey wearing matching gloss while giving him a blowjob shot an electric pulse down his spine. Too many thoughts like that and this would end much quicker than he'd planned.

He had to remain focused on Audrey to restrain the pending release. Clutching her ass, he pounded in and out of her. Her cries grew in volume as she twirled her hips, giving him the best lap dace of his life.

"I love watching you fuck Max, Audrey. But licking your pussy at the same time is the best dessert I could ask for."

Max groaned when Geoff's tongue swirled across his peritoneum, but when the evil man wrapped his tongue around one of his nuts, he almost lost it. "He's sucking on my balls now, Audrey." Her movements stuttered, proving what he'd already figured out. She liked a bit of dirty talk. "I bet he's jerking that thick cock of his while sucking on your pretty pink pussy."

"God, more...more...." Her body twitched in his arms.

"Damn right. I'm going to fill another condom when I come." Geoff's words were muffled against her pussy.

"Come all over his face, Audrey. Glaze his lips and cheeks with your cream and I'm going to lick him clean afterward."

She reached wildly for something to hold onto

while she panted, needy little noises rising in her throat. He caught one hand while Geoff held the other, anchoring her as they continued to manipulate her body. She cried out and rode him until he couldn't withstand his body's demands and followed her over into the abyss.

Though Max loved Geoff more than anything, he'd always known he had room in his heart for more than one. But until that moment, he hadn't really considered it would be a woman who'd share their bed. A firm believer in love at first sight, he'd known Audrey was meant for them as soon as they'd met. She lacked the shallow, superficial nature of the women they usually met, and her responses to their play weren't in the least bit bogus. His skull ached slightly where she'd gripped a fistful of his hair when she'd orgasmed, but the sated grin curling her lips made any pain worthwhile.

They'd barely had a moment to catch their breath when Max's cell rang. After fishing it out of his pants, Geoff handed it to him. A quick glance at the screen told Max it was one of the dealers from the casino.

"Good evening, Mr. Quinn. I wanted to let you know an impromptu private game is starting in forty-five minutes. Five hundred thousand to buy in, with a potential pot of three million."

The call stopped Max in his tracks. That kind of money would mean he wouldn't have to rely on Geoff to kick in the higher percentage for their projects. He could finally be an equal partner, and that kind of money would come in handy. He'd won practically the entire buy-in earlier, so that wouldn't be a problem.

"Where?"

That single word had Geoff whipping his head around to stare at him. His lover would know how much this meant to Max, but at the same time he could see Geoff's brows rise. Despite Geoff's very stable financial upbringing, he'd often been abandoned by his family because of some event or another. Audrey added a second layer of guilt. She wouldn't miss him—hell they hardly knew more than each other's first names. *But is this really how you want your life to be? Game to game, financial gain but losing Geoff's love over time?*

"Thanks for the call, George. I appreciate it, but I have plans for this evening that are more important."

"Did you win your game earlier?"

Max had been far too relaxed not to have won.

Geoff would easily admit he'd been concerned with the call about a private game. While they both understood winning wasn't guaranteed, for Geoff it had been less of a concern until recently. Max had begun jumping from game to game, and Geoff had grown concerned his lover had developed an addiction. A serious concern, since it would affect so much more than their immediate family. Relief poured through Geoff at hearing Max decline the dealer's invitation. Fear that the game they both enjoyed might destroy their future had been a black hole of worry in Geoff's thoughts for the last few months. Knowing that if they expanded their relationship to include Audrey, Max would be a responsible member of their trio, dissipated any black thoughts haunting Geoff.

"Won on a heart straight." Max pressed his lips against Audrey's temple. "I had no idea it would be a sign."

"How much was the pot?"

"Five hundred and fifty."

"I would have had a heart attack playing for that kind of money." Audrey shook her head like they were crazy. "That's more than half my rent for the month."

"*Thousand*, Audrey." Geoff gave her a half smile. "Max won five hundred and fifty thousand."

The moment the words left his mouth, he realized he'd made a vital error in judgment. Her eyes widened, and she paled. After finding out information like that, most women would have gotten a golden gleam in their eyes. Audrey had proven over and over she in no way resembled the gold-digging women they'd known.

"You were playing for over half a million dollars?" She pushed herself up, trying to put some space between them. "What if you had lost?"

"I wouldn't have been in such a good mood tonight." Max shrugged nonchalantly. "But when playing for that kind of money, you can't let it destroy you if you lose. It's part of the game."

"Do you know how much you could do to help people with that kind of money instead of playing games with it?"

The outrage in her tone surprised Geoff. He hadn't read her as some religious fanatic against gambling, but, somehow, he and Max had managed to hit a nerve.

"They can learn the game and play it, too, Audrey. It's not like it's an inherent gift. Playing poker is a

74

good way to make money, if you can handle the pressure."

The defensiveness in Max's voice originated from a man who'd worked hard to reach a higher echelon, but the naked woman between them didn't know that. "Audrey, he didn't mean it the way it sounded."

Max frowned. "Yes, I did."

"No, you didn't." Geoff glared, trying get his point across, but the idiot was being obtuse again.

Geoff wanted to strangle his boyfriend for being so thick-headed when Audrey crawled out from their embrace. Max's brain tended to go on hiatus after good sex, which hadn't been a problem, until now. She didn't acknowledge either of them as she fixed her dress, her flushed cheeks in contrast to her pale skin.

"Max, you owe her an explanation after that comment."

"I don't have to explain anything," Max said. "Hey, why are you getting dressed?"

"He doesn't owe me anything." She turned her attention to their lover and narrowed her gaze. "At least he doesn't throw money around like some high-and-mighty roller whose priorities are focused around his bank account."

"Who the hell—"

"Both of you stop right there!" Geoff lurched to his feet, grabbing for Audrey at the same time he tried to prevent falling over the pants still pooled at his feet.

A muffled snort sounded behind him, and Geoff glared at Max for a second time. "You'd better not be laughing at me, buddy"

Lips pressed tightly together and his eyes wide and full of mirth, Max shook his head in denial. Turning, Geoff caught Audrey with her hand over her mouth; apparently she fought a case of the giggles too. "*Eh tu*, Brute?"

"I'm sorry." Her voice rose a couple of octaves on the last word, which sent Max into gales of laughter.

Great, now I have to deal with two people with an affinity for slapstick humor. At least they weren't about to get into a fight started by a misunderstanding. Mustering up the tattered shreds of his dignity, Geoff yanked his pants up, adjusting so he didn't get caught in the zipper. "Now, that you both have had a good giggle, I'm not going to let assumptions ruin one of the best times of my life."

Audrey ran her fingers through her hair in an attempt to straighten it. He wanted to tell her that nothing would change the incredible, *just fucked* look she sported. The messy style looked good on her, and he could happily wake up to it every morning.

"Come here." He sat and tugged her hand, and she allowed him to lead her into his lap. She snuggled into him and rested her cheek on his chest. Amazingly, the silky tendrils of arousal stirred again, but his well-sated prick wasn't quite ready to play again. Max winced slightly when he moved, and Geoff winked at him. He'd reamed his partner's ass hard enough to make certain he'd feel it the rest of the night.

"I need a shower." Max crinkled his nose as he eased his pants up, and Geoff fought the urge to laugh at his lover's expense. "Not that I'm complaining." Max leaned over Audrey and licked the seam of Geoff's lips before claiming them. "Thank you, both." He brushed a kiss to her forehead and then gave her mouth the same gentle treatment. "We're lucky Geoff has a much clearer head after sex than I do. I didn't mean to be defensive."

"You're not the only one. I don't know anything about either of you, and I shouldn't have jumped to conclusions like that. It's just...that kind of money is more than I'll ever have and there is so much good you both could do with it." Shaking her head, she ran her fingers through her hair again. "But, I had no right to say what I did and I'm sorry if I sounded judgmental."

Max met his gaze. Geoff understood what his boyfriend wanted to do, and he nodded. Audrey was special. Call it poker instinct or simply a soul-deep desire, but he wanted to share something special with her, too.

"We'd like to show you something, Audrey. Something we've never told anyone else about.

Chapter Four

Audrey sat tucked between Geoff and Max in another taxi cab. She gave up fighting a yawn but tried to hide its intensity behind her forearm. After their last misunderstanding, she didn't want them to think they'd bored her with their big secret. She'd never imagined after only a few hours she could be so emotionally connected to one person let alone two.

"Ah, sweetheart, you're tired." Geoff tucked some hair behind her ear and brushed his thumb against her cheek. "Maybe this wasn't such a good idea after all."

"We've had better ideas," Max agreed and wrapped his arm around her, turning her face toward him. "I'd rather be in a cab on the way home with the intention of the three of us falling into bed and staying there for the next week." Much like in the club, his eyes were so dark they appeared black, but hints of gray flecks reflected the neon flashes passing by.

"That sounds like a great idea, but after we have our little field trip?" She hadn't meant for it to come out like a question, but a part of her didn't understand why they would choose her to reveal their secret to her.

Something caught her peripheral vision, and she stared past Max and out the window. "Oh my God, that's Sky!"

"Who?" they asked, but she'd twisted around to stare out the back window of the cab, too shocked to answer. Her peaceful, kind, infinitely patient friend was screaming like a banshee and waving her arms, her anger directed at two men over a head taller than her and built like The Hulk.

What if they hurt her? Sky was as harmless as a baby lamb.

"Stop the cab! We have to save her."

Then her delicate friend punched one of the giants in the solar plexus and kicked him in the balls. He doubled over and grabbed onto the other guy for balance before both toppled backward into a fountain. Audrey's jaw dropped in awe.

"I think she's okay." Geoff's words were almost drowned out by Max's laughter.

When the cab turned a corner, and she lost sight of Sky, Audrey didn't move, only continued to stare out the rear window.

"I'm sure she's fine. There's a crowd." Geoff rubbed her hip. "Nothing will happen to her."

Audrey turned and flopped down, already wondering if that had really been Sky or someone who only looked and dressed like her.

"Quite the hellion you have for a friend." Max wiped a tear from the corner of his eye as his laughter subsided. "Please introduce us one day."

Jealously flared, hot and unexpected, making Audrey's stomach cramp.

Geoff chuckled. "Because any woman who would tackle friggin' Special Forces is someone I'd like to have as a bodyguard."

Horror washed over Audrey. "What makes you think they're Special Forces?"

"I sat in on a poker game with them earlier today. They're both on an extended leave."

Audrey shuddered. "She's the gentlest soul I know and would make a terrible bodyguard. She doesn't even eat anything with a face."

"Too bad for those two guys then...." Max drawled.

"That's not funny, Max. We should call the cops. They must have been trying to attack her or they were lying to you and are con-artists or something."

Geoff snickered at Max's comment and hugged Audrey close. "Don't mind him. Haven't you figured out he has a warped sense of humor? You're the only woman we want guarding our bodies."

"I'll second that, and preferably naked." Max wiggled his eyebrows and bent his head to her chest. Cupping the underside of one breast through her dress, he lifted and nuzzled the skin he'd bared above her neckline.

"Sure, now you start, when we're almost there." Geoff stroked her leg.

She didn't dare look at the rearview mirror to see if the cabbie watched. Geoff's fingers curled under the hem of her dress. A few more inches, and he'd be close enough to stroke her pussy. Anticipation had her panting as they teased her. If they asked to fuck her there and then, she knew what her answer would be.

She jumped at a loud cough, followed by a throat clearing. The cabbie glanced back. "This is your stop."

"You should have taken us around the block a few

more times, my friend. You would have had a better show." Max handed a few bills to the driver. "Keep the change."

"Now you tell me! You have a beautiful woman. You like to share?"

Audrey glanced at the driver, who winked at her.

"Only with each other." Geoff helped Audrey out the back door.

Max said, "They're both mine."

Audrey blinked at the comment.

"He's possessive." Geoff whispered against her lips, "That growly tone of his always turns me on."

"I'm glad I'm not the only one." She laughed when Geoff wiggled his eyebrows at her. For the first time, she wasn't afraid to be silly with a man.

"Okay, you two. Geoff, you insisted she see this tonight. Let's give her a tour and then get home and into bed."

Audrey looked around. "Where are we?"

The glitz and sparkle of the main strip wasn't anywhere to be seen in the neighborhood the cab had taken them too. Garbage lay piled up along the side of the building in front of them, and the lack of lights hid whoever or whatever made shuffling noises in the alley. Unease skittered down her spin, and the plotline of a hundred horror movies flashed though her head. How many times had she gotten annoyed at women in movies who blindly went into dangerous situations and ended up dead? A weight stretched across her shoulders, making her jump.

"Hey, you okay?" Max shrugged out of his jacket and draped it over her shoulders. "You were holding yourself so tightly, I thought you were cold."

Audrey took a deep breath. "I'm a little nervous."

"I know what you mean. I always get nervous in this neighborhood, too." Geoff tangled his fingers with hers. "You'd better hold me tight. I might need protection."

Max rolled his eyes. "Smooth. If you wanted to hold her hand I'm sure you could have asked."

"No, really I'm scared," Geoff protested.

"You're full of it." Max leaned closer to him. "And, I promise, you'll be even fuller when I bury my cock in you later."

Audrey grinned at their silly banter, but the passionate embrace they shared reminded her of how much she wanted a repeat of what they'd done in the club.

"Come on, before I get too turned on and fuck you both in the alley." Max opened one of the doors in front of them.

Audrey hesitated for a moment, the idea of doing something as daring as sex in an alley had piqued her interest until the wind changed and she caught the nasty smell of urine emanating from it.

Max went in first, and Geoff held the door, and when she passed through, he swatted her playfully on the ass. When she walked in, she had no idea what to expect. The long stretches of tables lining the length of the room surprised her. The scent of coffee and biscuits hung in the air, and her stomach grumbled. It had been hours since dinner. A quick glance at her watch told her it was closer to breakfast.

"There's my boys!" An older woman came out from a back room with a tray of what smelled like apple tarts. She placed them on a counter next to a few other trays of baked goods. "It's been a while since you two were in this early. And who's your lady friend?

"Morning, Clarisse," Max and Geoff said simultaneously. They both gave the woman an affectionate peck on the cheek.

"We'd like you to meet our Audrey." Geoff tugged her forward, and she found herself under the scrutiny of a woman who didn't miss a thing, nor had she batted an eye when Geoff introduced her as *our Audrey*. Audrey wondered if this wasn't the first time Clarisse had heard that or it simply took a lot to ruffle her feathers. Audrey suspected the latter since Clarisse had the look of someone who'd had a hard life but still managed to smile.

Audrey's stomach took that moment to grumble again, and she rubbed it. "Oh God, I'm sorry."

"I don't believe you two." Clarisse slapped her ample hips. "Bringing this poor thing in here starving and then you wait to feed her by talking to me. Go sit, and I'll get you all something."

"Why don't you sit down and join us and let Max and I serve you for once?" Geoff asked.

"Because my baking is in the oven, and I don't want to ruin anything for the breakfast club." Clarisse shooed them away. "Go on, and I'll bring something out for you in a few minutes."

"You're busy enough. We'll get our own." Geoff pressed his hand to Audrey's lower back and led her over to the counter laden with carafes of coffee and trays of delicious-looking treats. As they picked out something to eat and got their coffees, a light chime sounded. The front door opened, and a man shuffled in. His clothes were ragged, but he smoothed down his greasy hair as he entered.

'Morn', Clari," the man mumbled and headed to one of the tables on the other side of the room. He pulled out a chair and made shooing motions as if brushing off an animal.

"Good morning, Jack. Apple or orange today?" Clarisse bustled over to a counter where dozens of bottles of orange and apple juice sat in a tub of ice water.

"Jack likes apple...."

"What is this place?" Audrey asked as Geoff led them to the end of one of the large tables. They settled on the bench seating, with her between the men.

"This is our place." Geoff waved his arm. "We try to feed as many street people as we can. There are three main meals offered at the same time every day, but Clarisse loves to bake, so she tends to start breakfast early. She has her favorites that she takes care of." He nodded in Jack's direction. "Jack's a bit of an odd guy and has been getting worse over the years, but, like many, he doesn't want help. No matter what, he always shows up here at this exact time every day, and Clarisse makes certain she gets one good meal into him."

"You wondered what we do with our money." Max gazed around the room, pride in his eyes. "This is the main reason I still play, aside from the fact that I enjoy the game."

Guilt slammed into Audrey; her earlier assumptions had been completely wrong. And then she'd made it worse by acting like a self-righteous bitch. This was the most wonderful, giving thing she'd ever witnessed. So many people talked about helping others and then made it a big production so everyone patted them on the back, but Max and Geoff had kept it a secret. They helped those in need because their hearts and priorities were in the right place. "I owe you both a massive apology. I shouldn't have said what I did."

"You don't owe us anything, Audrey. There are lots of greedy people in this town. We just try to do as much as we can."

"But we could do more if either of us had any business sense. This place sucks money like a black hole. Almost everyone here is a volunteer, although we try to take care of them as much as we can. We need a full-time manager who would know what the hell they were doing to run the place."

Audrey watched Clarisse taking care of Jake and

realized how important this place was to the neighborhood. Geoff poured cream and sugar into her coffee before she had a chance, and Max put a couple warm cinnamon buns on her plate. She'd wrongly thought the worst of them, but they hadn't held it against her.

Their date was supposed to be a one-night stand. She completely understood that, but the idea of never seeing Max and Geoff stabbed her in the heart like an ice pick.

"I don't want this to end." The words were out of her mouth before she had a chance to stop them. "I know we agreed to one night, but...." She couldn't finish. Because, if she told them she loved them, they'd laugh their asses off.

They each took one of her hands in their own, but she wouldn't look at either man. They'd already proven they were too observant and would know how she felt because she didn't have any clue how to hide it. Telling them she loved them after only a few hours was crazy. *Wasn't it?*

"This has been the most intense and perfect night of our lives." Geoff sounded so sincere. She peeked up at him, fearing she'd see some sort of amusement on his face. "I'd like to think that this was some sort of love at first sight but I don't believe in that."

"I do." Max claimed her attention with the two simple words. "I don't want you to say anything right now, Audrey. But I know how I feel and who I need, and that's both you and Geoff in my bed, every night. But, Geoff's right. This has been an intense and wild night, and I want you to make certain we're what you want."

How she wanted to holler *Yes*! Instead, they took turns kissing her, preventing her from saying anything until Clarisse came over and gave them both hell for not letting Audrey eat.

Sitting between them, she nibbled bits of sticky cinnamon buns from their fingers and took turns feeding them. A soul-deep calm settled over her as she sat at the scratched-up table in a Vegas soup kitchen. Flanked by the two most beautiful and thoughtful men she'd ever met, she knew she was where she was meant to be.

Epilogue

The hot Jamaican sun hung high in the cloudless sky, warming Audrey. She'd been careful to put on enough sunscreen earlier, but her skin had started to tingle under the sun's rays, especially the pale parts usually hidden away.

"Don't stay out there too much longer. I don't want you to burn."

She smiled at the concern in Max's voice. There'd been a time when she'd thought she'd be all alone in her life. Now she had not one, but two incredible men she loved with every cell in her body. There'd been a time when the thought of being out in the sunshine in a bathing suit could have sent her into a panic attack. Lately...she didn't even bother with the suit.

Geoff and Max had taken her on a surprise vacation to the Caribbean. Supposedly, the beach was private, but people tended to wander by every so often, which had helped to encourage her exhibitionist side. Arching, she pressed her chest up and stretched like a lazy feline.

A shadow fell over her, blocking the sun's heated caress. "Hey, buddy, you're blocking my rays."

"Really?" Geoff drawled. Bending slightly, he shook his head, splattering her with water, the cold droplets a sharp contrast to her hot skin. When she squealed and tried to escape, he dropped down and pinned her under him on the chaise lounge she'd been relaxing in.

"I think you were deliberately teasing us."

"I never tease, and you're all wet." She wriggled under him, the hard ridge of his erection rubbing deliciously against her clit. He slipped a hand under her ass and supported her, giving him the perfect angle to push into her.

"So are you." Her body stretched to accommodate his girth, stealing her breath. Lying outside, naked for anyone to see had kept her wet, on edge, and primed for the men's' touch. She wrapped her legs around him, and Geoff rewarded her by snapping his hips back before plunging into her again.

"I could watch you both all day."

Geoff pressed deep and stilled when his crown tapped her cervix. He turned his gaze beside them; Audrey followed it to find Max leaning against one of the pillars that supported the pagoda covering the deck. The sun glinted off his black hair and highlighted his muscles. He lazily stroked his cock while watching them. It had taken some time, but she'd begun to understand why they liked to show off. She couldn't deny the feeling of power she claimed when playing to their voyeuristic tendencies.

Crooking a finger, she asked, "Why don't you come over here?"

Max slowly shook his head, continuing to pump into his fist. "Don't stop on my account."

"Tell us what you've decided." Geoff toyed with her clit, lighting up her nerve endings like fireworks, but it wasn't the intense friction she craved.

Smacking his shoulder, she dug her heels into his ass and tried to get Geoff to shift, but he refused so she rhythmically clenched her vaginal muscles against his length.

"Fuck, God that feels good." Geoff invaded her mouth, tangling his tongue with hers before pulling back. "Don't tease, tell us."

Audrey almost fell for it, but couldn't prevent the

laugh that escaped at his pouty, sad face. There was nothing better than a good laugh in the middle of great sex. "Yes, you crazy men, I quit my job at the soul-sucking hellhole."

A heartbeat later, Max knelt next to the lounger, kissing her with every bit of passion that Geoff had. Sliding her hand up, she rolled his balls in her palm, and Geoff joined her, wrapping his fingers around Max's cock. She loved to watch the men and witness the love they shared. She couldn't believe they'd welcomed her into their lives so quickly.

"You're staying with us?" Max lifted his face to stare at her.

"Yes." She'd decided to quit her job the moment her plane had lifted off, taking her away from her men. Leaving them that first time had been the hardest thing she'd ever done. When she'd received the email from them inviting her on a holiday two days later, she'd already given notice and made arrangements with Clarisse to take over the business aspect of running the soup kitchen. They needed organization and someone to figure out the financial side of things, something well within her experience and talents.

"Good. I love you so much, I planned to hide your

passport if you tried to say no." Max smiled, his eyes looking a bit misty, and she suspected hers did, too.

"For the rest of our lives?"

She met Geoff's gorgeous eyes and smiled. "I'll love you both, forever."

He grinned in return, slowly plunging into her body while she encouraged Max to lean over her, drawing his cock into her mouth and sucking his length to the back of her throat.

A loud gasp sounded from somewhere closer to the beach, ramping up their combined arousal. Her men's exhibitionistic tendencies were rubbing off on her, and she wouldn't have it any other way.

Audrey had taken a chance on love, laid her cards on the table, and found herself in the middle of a royal flush—a Queen of Hearts between her Noble King and Wild Joker.

About the Author

Best selling author Kayleigh Malcom (and her alter ego Corinne Davies) is a firm believer that all love is beautiful and everyone deserves a Happily Ever After....well except for those involved with cancelling Firefly. She's still holding a grudge over that one.

She first put pen to paper in an attempt to write a love story between her and her favourite rock singer of the time. It was filled with all the angst that only a teenager can come up with and, of course, an incredible wardrobe. Years later, during the wee hours of the morning, when her first daughter insisted on waking up, she discovered online RPGs and her love of writing emerged again.After many encouraging words from fellow writers, she decided to try her hand at developing her own stories, learning it takes more than mind blowing sex and a happily ever after to make a great story.

By day, she is a full-time wife, mother, and product consultant. At night, she avoids such mundane tasks as housework and laundry by creating her own worlds where fantasy and mythology comes to life. Worlds in which you are just as likely to be living next door to an ancient Deity as finding your soul mate in steam powered flying machine. Sticking with one genre is a talent she hasn't achieved yet and can be found creating worlds as normal as our own or as fantastic as her dreams. Her characters have to face real life challenges, as many of us do, but love always finds a way to conquer all.

A social media junkie, she can be found haunting many different sites and loves to hear from her readers.

www.ingramcontent.com/pod-product-compliance
Lightning Source LLC
Chambersburg PA
CBHW070637130626
46555CB00006B/2586